Let fear disapp...

THE SLIME SQUAD

is here!

Evil nose-monsters are attacking
Trashland. The Squad must
fight back ...

It's time to fight crime with slime!

Collect all the cool cards and check out
the special website for more slimy stuff:

www.slimesquad.co.uk

Don't miss the rest of the series:

THE SLIME SQUAD VS THE FEARSOME FISTS
THE SLIME SQUAD VS THE TOXIC TEETH
THE SLIME SQUAD VS THE SUPERNATURAL SQUID
THE SLIME SQUAD VS THE CYBER-POOS
THE SLIME SQUAD VS THE KILLER SOCKS
THE SLIME SQUAD VS THE LAST-CHANCE CHICKEN
THE SLIME SQUAD VS THE ALLIGATOR ARMY

Also available by the same author, these
fantastic series:

COWS IN ACTION

ASTROSAURS

ASTROSAURS ACADEMY

www.stevecolebooks.co.uk

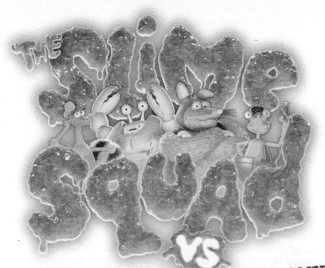

THE SLIME SQUAD

vs

THE CONQUERING CONKS

by Steve Cole

Illustrated by Woody Fox

RED FOX

SLIME SQUAD vs THE CONQUERING CONKS
A RED FOX BOOK 978 1 849 41402 9

First published in Great Britain by Red Fox,
an imprint of Random House Children's Publishers UK
A Random House Group Company

This edition published 2012

1 3 5 7 9 10 8 6 4 2

The Random House Group Limited supports the Forest Stewardship
Council (FSC®), the leading international forest certification
organization. Our books carrying the FSC label are printed on FSC®-
certified paper. FSC is the only forest certification scheme endorsed by
the leading environmental organizations, including Greenpeace. Our
paper procurement policy can be found at
www.rbooks.co.uk/environment.

MIX
Paper from
responsible sources
FSC
www.fsc.org   FSC® C016897

Set in16/20pt Bembo Schoolbook by
Falcon Oast Graphic Art Ltd

Red Fox Books are published by
Random House Children's Publishers UK,
61–63 Uxbridge Road, London W5 5SA

www.**randomhousechildrens**.co.uk
www.**totallyrandombooks**.co.uk
www.**randomhouse**.co.uk

Addresses for companies within The Random House Group Limited can
be found at: www.randomhouse.co.uk/offices.htm

THE RANDOM HOUSE GROUP Limited Reg. No. 954009

A CIP catalogue record for this book is available from
the British Library.

Printed in the UK by CPI Group (UK) Ltd, Croydon, CR0 4YY

For Ann Giles
The most wicked Bookwitch

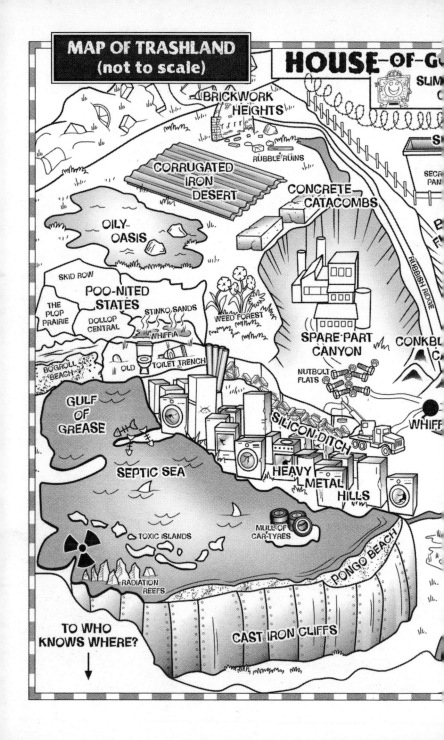

ONCE UPON A SLIME...

The old rubbish dump was far from anywhere. An enormous, mucky, rusty landscape of thousands of thrown-away things.

It had been closed for years. Abandoned. Forgotten.

And then Godfrey Gunk came along.

Godfrey wasn't just a mad scientist. He was a SUPER-BONKERS scientist! And he was very worried about the amount of pollution and rubbish in the world. His dream was to create marvellous mutant mini-monsters out of chemical goo – monsters who would clean up the planet by eating, drinking and generally devouring all types of trash. So Godfrey bought the old rubbish dump as the perfect testing-ground and got to work.

Of course, he wanted to make good, friendly, peaceful monsters, so he was careful to keep the nastiest, most toxic chemicals separate from the rest. He worked for years and years . . .

And got nowhere.

In the end, penniless and miserable, Godfrey wrecked his lab, scattered his experiments all over the dump, and moved away, never to return.

But what Godfrey didn't know was that long ago, tons of radioactive sludge had been accidentally dumped there. And soon, its potent powers kick-started the monster chemistry the mad scientist had tried so hard to create!

Life began to form. Amazing mini-monsters sprang up with incredible speed. Bold, inventive monsters, who made a wonderful, whiffy world for themselves from the rubbish around them – a world they named Trashland.

For many years, they lived and grew in peace. But then the radiation reached a lead-lined box in the darkest corner of the rubbish dump – the place where Godfrey had chucked the most toxic, dangerous gunk of all.

Slowly, very slowly, monsters began to grow here too.

Different monsters.

Evil monsters that now threaten the whole of Trashland.

Only one force for good stands against them. A small band of slightly sticky superheroes . . .

The Slime Squad!

Chapter One

MORNING OF MYSTERIES

Early-rising monsters were the first to notice the message in the sky. It had appeared mysteriously overnight, hanging high over the whiffy streets of Trashland in big smoky letters. Within minutes, masses more monsters were gazing out of windows or gathering in the streets, wondering what the words meant:

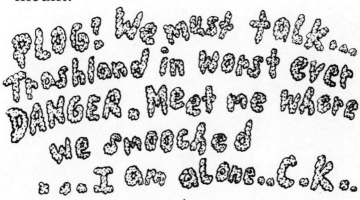

PLOG! We must talk... Trashland in worst ever DANGER. Meet me where we smooched ...I am alone..C.K..

1

Monsters everywhere knew that Plog was the shaggy leader of the Slime Squad – those super-cool superheroes who kept Trashland safe from diabolical masterminds. But who would leave such an extravagant message? What *was* the danger?

And –YUCK! – who exactly had been smooching with Plog . . . ?

"Attention!" The electronic bark of the All-Seeing PIE echoed through the Slime Squad's secret underground base. "Come to my office. Let's be having you! SHIFT YOURSELVES!"

"All right, all right!" Plog rolled out of his padded-envelope bed and checked the time. "It's not even six o'clock in the morning!"

PIE, short for Perfect Intelligent Electronics, was the brains behind the Slime Squad. He was a mega-computer with sensors scattered all over Trashland, perfectly placed to spot trouble brewing – and when he did, he tipped off the Squad and sent them to deal with it.

Something dangerous must be kicking off, thought Plog.

He barged out of his bedroom and hurried along the corridor to PIE's office, an enormous, messy, human-sized room. The battered computer sat right in the middle, his screen bright green and covered in exclamation marks.

"Look out of the window!" PIE snapped.

Plog's jaw dropped as he saw the cloudy message in the sky. It dropped so far it almost bounced off the waterlogged boots he wore at all times – for  whenever his feet were dry, disgusting slime oozed out with a pong strong enough to knock out a nuclear gibbon.

"First smooch?" he spluttered. "Who's C.K.? I don't understand. That message must be meant for another Plog."

"I don't think so, Fur-boy." Zill Billie, a black-and-white she-monster, had swung into the room on a strand of sticky slime. Part poodle, part skunk,

4

with six legs and a big brushy tail, she
was the Squad's super-cool slime-slinger
– and right now she was wearing pink
pyjamas and a very worried look.
"When I see the letters C.K. together,
someone very nasty springs to mind."

As Zill spoke, a yellow frog-monster
in big metal pants and a crash helmet
sprang into the room – it was Furp
LeBurp, the chemistry whizz whose
slimy hands and feet let him stick to
any surface. "C.K., you say?" He
jumped onto the window and stuck

there, peering out.
"Good gonkberries, it
simply *has* to be her,
doesn't it?"

"Has to be who?"
Plog demanded.

"How could you
forget the monster who almost
smooched you to death, Plog?" said PIE
tetchily. "This message in the sky must
have been left by . . . Countess Kiss!"

"Oh, no!" Plog slapped his forehead
so hard he almost fell over. "How could
I forget *that* ratbag?"

An old picture of Countess Kiss
appeared on PIE's cracked screen: she
was tall, thin and bony, wearing a white
raincoat, her clawed hands resting on
her hips. In place of a face she had an
enormous pair of lips, with two little
green eyes perched on top. Hoop
earrings (or rather *lip*-rings) dangled
down at either side.

Plog shuddered at the memory of their first meeting. The countess had snogged his snout with breath so stinky it almost melted his brain! "We haven't seen her since we stopped her toxic tooth-monster," he murmured. "I wonder what she wants?"

"It's a trick, I'll bet," Zill declared.

Furp nodded. "If there's a danger to Trashland it's most likely her and those Gruesome Gobs who serve her – Sukka and Blowdart."

"Incorrect," PIE warbled. The picture on his screen changed to show a short film of a red blob and a blue blob with battered suitcases running up a sludgy hillside until they vanished from sight.

"Sukka and Blowdart left Trashland in a rush last Thursday, heading east over the Gunk Glaciers towards the human world. They have not returned."

Zill shook her head, and her pom-poms wobbled. "Countess Kiss and the Gruesome Gobs were one mean team. Why would the Gobs split without their mistress?"

"Perhaps she tried to snog *them*," Plog suggested.

"My sensors have detected many other dangerous monsters leaving Trashland," PIE revealed. "The Fearsome Fists you fought fled last Wednesday. A bunch of Maggot Men moved out last Monday." He flashed up a picture of something fierce and blobby with fifteen bottoms and one leg. "And I have no idea what *this* thing is, but it hopped out of Trashland's Darkest Corner two days ago."

"Why are so many bad guys leaving?" wondered Plog, turning back to the window. "I mean, I'm glad to see the back of them, but what's made them go?"

"Countess Kiss may have the answers," said PIE. "You must meet her as she asks – as soon as Danjo arrives."

Zill looked around for the fourth and final Squaddie. "Is he still asleep?"

"No," said PIE, "he is upgrading the Slime-mobile's engines and steering systems."

"All done!" Danjo Jigg, a crimson crab-monster, swaggered in. He was covered in oil. "Let me freshen up and I'll be right with you." Holding up his big left pincer, he doused himself with steaming hot slime, then blasted his body with a spray of icy slime from his right pincer. "Brrr, that's better!" Clean again, he beamed round at his friends.

"I thought I heard PIE's alarm go off while I was tuning the turbo booster. What's up . . . ?" He trailed off as he saw the message through the window. "Oh, NO! Must be from that lippy old miss – Countess Kiss!"

"And I have just spied her," PIE said proudly. "She is sitting in a box in the alleyway beside the Dentists-R-Us building in Spare Part Canyon."

"That's where we first met her, all right," Plog confirmed. "Can you show us?"

The scene on PIE's screen shifted once again – to reveal the countess, half-hidden by cardboard, looking very sorry for herself. Her raincoat was torn and dirty, her lips looked chapped, and her green eyes were full of tears.

"She looks a mess!" Zill shook her head. "What's happened to her?"

"Wait!" PIE squawked suddenly. "More importantly – *what* has happened to the Nosepick Ocean?" His screen flicked to show a filthy beach beside a thick, pale-green sea.

"This is a view from the Car Wreck Coast. The level of the Nosepick Ocean has dropped by more than half overnight – without explanation. And my sensors detect it is *still* going down."

Suddenly – SQUELCH! The screen went dark.

"Warning!" warbled PIE. "Vision-booster in the Car Wreck Coast zone has stopped working. All sight sensors in that area are now off-line."

"Sorry, PIE. No peeking." A harsh voice crackled through PIE's speakers, quickly followed by rasping laughter. "And *now* say goodbye to your electronic ears . . ."

The line crackled and went silent.

"Noooo!" PIE's screen shone neon red. "Audio circuits destroyed. I can no longer see or hear anything around the Car Wreck Coast!"

"But no one in Trashland knows about you or your sensors." Furp looked worried. "How did they find out that you were watching them?"

"I don't know," PIE admitted. "Zill, Furp, Danjo – you must investigate at once."

"What about me?" Plog looked puzzled. "Aren't I going with them?"

"Only as far as Spare Part Canyon," said PIE gravely. "You have a date to keep – with Countess Kiss!"

Chapter Two

SNIFFING OUT TROUBLE

Waving 'bye to PIE, the Squaddies raced off to the garage where the Slime-mobile – their invisible, super-charged transport – stood ready, its doors open.

Plog sighed as he bundled his friends aboard and grabbed a golden mask from the costume store. "I wish I was coming with you guys to get whoever broke PIE's sensor."

"We wish we were coming with *you* in case Lady Lippy's pulling a fast one," said Danjo, changing into his golden shorts.

"PIE knows best, I suppose," said Furp, swapping his stainless steel pants for a gleaming golden pair with a helmet to match. "You must take a trash-taxi to join us as soon as you've heard what the countess has to say."

Zill pulled off her PJs and slipped on her golden leotard, ready for action. "We'll most likely be there and back in time to pick you up," she said, taking the driver's seat, "now that Danjo's fitted this extra-strong turbo booster to the engines."

"Test it on quarter-power first," Danjo advised. "I'm not quite sure just how fast it can go."

"Meanwhile, how about a little breakfast as we drive, for extra strength?" Furp headed for his lav-lab in the vehicle's rear, which was part laboratory, part toilet and all whiffy. "I've been experimenting with some old  human food I found in the base's kitchen." He held up a bowl of orange gunk. "Look! This is human slime called ketchup mixed with stuff called vinegar and mustard—"

But then Zill hit the turbo button, and the Slime-mobile shot forward at spectacular speed. "Woo-hooo!" she cheered.

Furp lost his balance and his bowl of runny goo splashed into Danjo's face.

"Urgh!" Danjo spluttered, wiping his eyes. "I can't see."

"Probably just as well." Plog watched the world outside whizz past in a blur and clung to Furp's lab bench for dear life. "Saves you having to hide your eyes!"

"We'd better make breakfast brief," said Furp, grabbing two jars. "Boiled earwig legs, anyone? They're even tastier with some of this brown dust humans call pepper . . ."

As he offered them round, Zill took a corner at a hundred miles an hour. He fell over and threw the pepper all over Plog's long snout.

The powder prickled and tickled Plog's nostrils, and then – "AAAA–CHOO!" He started to sneeze with the force of a small typhoon! "Ugh, this stuff is seriously sneeze-worthy. AA-CHOO! KER-*CHOO*!" He blew the earwig legs off the plate and straight up Furp's nose!

19

"OWW!" cried Furp, tumbling backwards into the toilet with a SPLOSH – just as Zill hit the brakes and the Slime-mobile hiccupped to a halt.

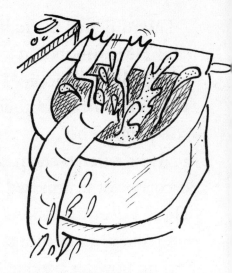

"First stop, Fur-boy – Dentists-R-Us, Spare Part Canyon." Zill turned to her friends – and frowned to see Danjo covered in sauce, Plog blowing his nose with a face-full of pepper and Furp's feet sticking out of the lav. "Um . . . everything all right back there?"

"Just great." Plog sneezed again and nodded. "Thanks for breakfast, Furp."

"You're welcome," Furp called weakly from the loo.

"Good luck with the countess, Plog," said Zill.

Danjo wiped his face and nodded. "Tell her from us – if she causes you trouble, we'll turn her to rubble!"

Plog smiled gratefully. "Just take care when you reach the Nosepick Ocean. Those clowns who messed with PIE's sensors sounded tough." He opened the door and stepped out onto a wide street made of rusty metal; it was still so early that no one was in sight. "I'll join you there as soon as I've found out what that message in the sky is all about."

But as the Slime-mobile zoomed off in a cloud of invisible smoke, Plog's heart felt heavy. He had a feeling that there was big trouble ahead – bigger than any the Squad had yet encountered . . .

"So," came a soft, breathy voice behind him. "Your friends have left you – just like mine have run out on me."

Plog turned to see the ragged, sinister figure of Countess Kiss huddled in the alley beside the huge dentists' building.

"My friends have *not* left me," Plog retorted. "It's just that they have a bigger problem than you to deal with right now."

The countess shushed him. "Keep your voice down and let's talk in the alley where no one can see us."

"Trying to lead me into a trap, huh?" Plog shook his head. "Forget it – I can smell that breath of yours from over here. You can say whatever you want to say out in the open!"

"Please . . . I mustn't be seen." She limped back into the shadows and looked around anxiously. "*They* are after me."

"Who?" Plog demanded. "What's going on?"

"I'll tell you everything." Countess Kiss took a deep breath. "But first you must promise to give me the Slime Squad's protection."

"Protection?" Plog almost burst out laughing. "You're a big-time baddie! Why should we protect you?"

"Oh, don't call me bad, Ploggy-Woggy," purred the countess. "I was just a bored, silly dentist who fell in with the wrong crowd."

"Well, if you think you can get close to *my* crowd, forget it. We know you're up to something." Plog pointed to the fading words in the sky. "Was that message meant to distract us from whatever's draining the Nosepick Ocean?"

"Nose . . . pick . . . ?" Countess Kiss echoed, the colour draining from her lips. "Oh no. It must be *them* again." She ran back down the alley, jumped into a cardboard box and sat there quivering.

24

"You really *are* frightened, aren't you?" Plog murmured. "Why?"

"I told you — *they* are after me," the countess whimpered. "First, *they* drove all the bad guys out of the Murky Badlands and the Darkest Corner — even my Gruesome Gobs — so that no one could hatch any evil schemes to rival theirs. Now, *they* are getting ready to attack our world . . ."

"They?" Plog frowned. "Who *are* 'they'?"

A second later — SPLAT! A bright green lump exploded on the alley wall beside Plog's head.

"Get down!" The countess leaped out of her box and pounced on Plog, pulling him to the pavement. He started to gasp at the pong of her breath – then gasped louder as two more sizzling green bursts struck the spot where he'd been standing moments earlier.

"You saved me from a splatting!" Plog frowned at the countess. "Then . . . you really aren't trying to trick me?"

"Not that it matters now." Countess Kiss burst into tears. "*They* have found me. *They* are here!"

Plog looked past her trembling, oversized lips to see a bulky figure sniffing and snuffling through the alley shadows. It was large, pink and knobbly, and covered in spots. It had two spindly arms, three hairy legs and a mean-looking mouth. Mad eyes stared out from beneath thick, bristly brows. On either side of its bulbous body, a round, dark hole was dribbling green goo.

"It . . . it looks like a *nose*," breathed Plog in disbelief. "A giant walking nose."

The nightmare nose-creature's eyes narrowed. "Do not move," it rasped in a cold, bunged-up voice. "Countess Kiss . . . Plog of the Slime Squad . . . from this moment, you are powerless prisoners of the all-conquering Conks!"

Snorting and wheezing, the bizarre beast lumbered towards them.

Chapter Three

UP TO NOSE GOOD

"Sorry to disappoint you, Nosy," said Plog, still lying sprawled on the alley floor, "but the Slime Squad's leader is *never* powerless!" He kicked the empty cardboard box into the conk-monster's face.

"Fool!" With a snarl and a swipe of its three-fingered hand, the creature batted the box away. "Soggy cardboard cannot stop us."

"But it can buy me time to get back in the *ring*!" Plog had tugged out one of the countess's gold hoops, and now he hurled it at the Conk's left eye. The giant nose snorted in pain and staggered backwards.

"Now I see why you wanted protection." Plog jumped up and grabbed Countess Kiss by the wrist. "I'd quite like some myself – come on, run!"

The unlikely allies sprinted to the end of the passage – only to find three more creepy conk-creatures hurrying towards them, blocking their escape route.

"I've heard of running noses, but this is ridiculous!" Plog dragged Countess Kiss up the front steps of the Dentists-R-Us building and shoulder-charged the heavy door, smashing it open. "Come on, we'll hide inside." More green splats sprayed the wall beside them. "Ugh – they're firing nose-juice out of their nostrils!"

"Don't let it touch you," Countess Kiss warned him. "That revolting stuff is what scared away poor Sukka and Blowdart. If it hits you, you'll be at the Conks' mercy – and they don't have any!"

Plog ducked as another gooey missile flew over his head. "We'd better run for it." He charged into a showroom full of dentist's chairs and headed for the back stairs, Countess Kiss close behind him. As they took the steps three at a time, the horrendous hooters burst into the building, firing wildly.

"No wonder they sound so bunged up," Plog panted. "They must have never-ending snot supplies!"

A sign at the top of the staircase announced the MOUTHWASH DEPARTMENT. Big bottles of minty antiseptic were stacked up all around; Plog quickly knocked them over and kicked them down the stairs, directly into the path of the rampaging Conks. They snarled and snorted as they were sent flying, banging and crashing out of sight.

MOUTHWASH
DEPARTMENT

"That won't stop
them for long," the
countess panted. "Keep
moving."

Plog sprinted with her up
the next flight of stairs and
followed her out onto the roof.
To his surprise, a small white
aircraft was parked there. A lipsticky
kiss-mark was printed on each pointed
wing and a large exhaust pipe hung
down from its rear.

"Your own private aircraft," Plog
realized. "So *that's* how you left the
smoke-writing in the sky."

33

"Naturally." Countess Kiss ran over to the plane and opened the door. "I suppose that since I want your friends to help protect me, I'd better not abandon you to the Conks. Climb aboard."

"You're too kind," Plog muttered, squeezing into the seat beside her as she started the engine. The plane's propellers began to spin — just as the Conks burst out onto the rooftop. Plog's tummy lurched as the plane took to the air amid a hailstorm of gooey green missiles, climbing quickly out of range.

"Phew," said Plog. "We got away."

"But they'll keep coming after us," Countess Kiss sighed. "They've already chased me halfway across Trashland. Now it seems they want you as well."

"I wonder *why* these Conks want to capture us? Why not just drive us away like they did all the bad guys – or simply kill us?" Plog frowned. "Where did they come from, anyway? How many are there?"

"Who knows?" said the countess. "But you heard for yourself what they're planning to do. They want to conquer Trashland!"

Plog remembered the bunged-up boast of the nasty nose all too well – then realized its voice was the same as whatever had scrunched PIE's sensors that morning. "There must be more of these weird conk-creatures up to no good on the Car Wreck Coast," he muttered. "Maybe lots more."

Countess Kiss shrugged. "So?"

"So that means Zill, Furp and Danjo are in massive danger," said Plog. "We've got to get to them – fast!"

At that exact moment, Zill, Furp and Danjo were bouncing through the vast rust-and-rubber outskirts of the Car Wreck Coast. The crumpled cars had once belonged to human giants, and were slowly falling apart in titanic, teetering heaps. Beside them, the Nosepick Ocean shifted sludgily in the morning breeze.

Furp looked out of the window. Judging by the thick, sticky slime-trails over much of the metal coastline, the sea-level was dropping fast. "Brake here, Zill, could you?"

he called. "I think
we're nearing the
spot where PIE's
sensors are hidden."

Zill slowed the
Slime-mobile to a
trundle and checked
the electronic map
beside her. "You're right.
There should be two human-car tyres
on top of each other somewhere round
here – PIE's sensors are squeezed in
between them."

"I can't understand why it's so quiet."
Danjo peered around. "There's a
Formula Bum motor race being held
near here today. There should be loads
of monsters getting ready."

"It's still early, remember," said Furp,
"and we've come in on the back roads."
But secretly he was feeling quite
unnerved himself. None of them had
spied a single monster. And since PIE's

sensors had been destroyed, even their big boss couldn't warn them of any possible dangers. "The sooner I repair PIE's bits and pieces, the better."

"That must be the place." Zill drove towards a pair of large, dirty tyres on top of a hillside of broken car doors. "Let's check it out."

Zill stopped the Slime-mobile beside the tyres. Furp hopped straight out and scaled the metal tower to inspect the damage. "Ah-ha," he murmured, catching sight of an aerial sticking out between the two tyres. Then he saw that the electronics beneath were covered in a thick green goo, hardening in the sunshine. "Yuck!"

"What is it?" Zill called up to him.

"I'm not sure." Furp pulled out a screwdriver from his pants and prodded the sticky mess. "Some kind of slime, I think." But when he tried to tug the screwdriver out again, he found he couldn't. "It's like a kind of green glue, gumming up the works. I'll have to mix up something in the lav-lab that will dissolve it."

"That's going to take you some time, right?" Danjo looked at Zill. "While Furp's busy, why don't we climb the hill and see if we can spot anyone?"

Zill nodded. "Will you be all right on your own for a bit, Furp?"

"Sure," said Furp. "But be careful."

He watched his friends charge away up the hill, the sun flashing off their golden outfits, then wriggled through the gap between the tyres to inspect PIE's gummed-up sensors more closely.

"YOU are the one who should be careful," came a thick, bunged-up voice above him.

"What—?" Furp looked up to find a huge, lumpy nose-monster jumping down from the rim of the tyre above him. "Ooof!" The thing knocked him flying and he fell to the ground with a thump. Stunned for a second, Furp heard the nose land beside him, sniffing and snorting.

"You shouldn't be so nosy," it said.
"That's *our* job . . ."

And the next thing Furp
knew, a giant quivering
nostril was closing
around his head! It
was hot, dark and
sticky. Sharp hairs
scratched his froggy
skin. Slimy goo
bubbled around
his face. "I can't
breathe!" he
gasped. "Zill!
Danjo, help!"

"Zill Billie and
Danjo Jigg are not
required," rasped the monster. "Only you
and your leader are needed to help the
Conks!"

Then Furp's eyes flickered shut and he
knew no more . . .

Chapter Four
TISSUE ATTACK!

Unaware of the fate that had befallen their friend, Zill and Danjo were clambering over the car wrecks that made up the local coastline. The rusty ground clinked and crumbled under their feet.

"I think the racetrack is on the other side of these huge cars," said Danjo. "How about we take a short cut?" Raising his right pincer, he sprayed a stream of slush out in an arch, right over the roof of a giant vehicle. It quickly hardened to ice and Danjo climbed over it like a bridge.

"Good thinking, partner!" Zill spat a slime-line at Danjo's back, sat down on the ice and held on, allowing him to tow her to the top.

The two Squaddies were soon gazing down over a monster racetrack, crammed with sporty motors and crowds of onlookers. "That's more like it," said Danjo. "They're all getting ready for the race."

"But then . . . how come no one's moving?" Zill stared around, baffled. "It's like they're playing musical statues — and forgot to bring any music."

"What are we going to do?" wailed a mattress-mite in the crowd.

An old man monster beside her nodded. "I'm so hungry and thirsty . . ."

"And I really need the toilet," groaned one of the drivers from inside his car.

"What's the matter with them all?" Danjo wondered.

"I'm not sure. But they look afraid." Zill bunched her fists. "Well, let fear disappear . . ."

"The Slime Squad is here!" Danjo clapped his pincers together. "Or half of it, anyway."

Zill slid down the other side of the frozen bridge like a champion speed-skater, while Danjo followed close behind.

"Look!" The mattress-mite pointed but didn't budge from where she stood. "The Slime Squad are coming!"

"They'll save us!" cried the old man monster.

"Have they brought a potty?" called the driver.

"Unstick us!" a big, three-eyed lady monster begged. "Please, set us free!"

"What are they on about?" Zill
muttered as she hurried over. Then she
saw the puddles. They were nasty, thick
and green, and the monsters were
stuck in them up to their
ankles. The cars were
held tight too.

"Furp said that green glue was
gumming up PIE's sensors, didn't he?"
Gingerly, Zill put a paw against the goo
– and had to fight to free it again.
"Where did this stuff come from?"

"The noses!" moaned the mattress-
mite.

Danjo scratched his head. "The
who?"

"Revolting conk-creatures," the old man monster confirmed. "In place of nostrils they have double-barrelled snot-guns."

"We got here early for the races, and they ambushed us," said the three-eyed monster. "First their servants rounded us up. Then the noses stuck us to the ground with their hooter-juice."

"I guess that must be what they didn't want PIE to see." Zill's own nose wrinkled. "Why would these conk-creatures do this? And where are they now?"

"I think they went off to round up some more victims," said the mattress-mite. "They could be back at any time."

"Sounds crazy," said Danjo, "but I guess it's *snot* to be laughed at."

An excited buzz of chatter was swelling as the trapped monsters realized they might be close to rescue. "Please, everyone, shh!" Zill called as loudly as she dared. "The things that did this to you might hear and come straight back!"

Danjo tried to lift the lady monster clear – but she could not be budged. He fired red-hot slime at the sludgy stuff, but it had no effect. Zill helped him,

pulling so hard that the lady monster began to stretch like chewing gum! But finally, after five minutes of frantic pulling – *FRRRRRIP!* – she came loose. "Thank you!" she groaned.

"You're welcome," Zill panted. "But if we take that long to free everyone, it'll take us months!"

"Months?" said the red-faced racing-car driver. "Oh, no. I really *do* need a wee!"

Zill saw that his doors and windows had been glued shut by more of the sticky splats, trapping him inside. She coughed up a slime-line and spat it at the back of the car. "Danjo, let's try to pull him out – then we can use his car to help us tow more monsters to safety."

The two Squaddies heaved and strained with all their strength. Then, suddenly, something wispy and white

caught Zill's eye, blowing over the top of Danjo's ice bridge. It hung there for a few moments like a kind of sheet, until another one blew against it. Then both floated down towards the racetrack.

"EEEEEK!" The lady monster ran for her life and the crowd erupted in panic. They gasped and yelped and screamed, waving their arms and wobbling about, desperately trying to free themselves.

Zill frowned. "Shush, you lot!" she hissed as the white things wafted over and brushed against Danjo's legs. "It's only a couple of old tissues."

"You don't understand!" The old man monster's eyes were wide with fright. "Those are no ordinary tissues – they are *servants to the noses!*"

Even as he spoke, the tissues tightened
and twisted around Danjo's three sturdy
legs with savage force. "Hey!" cried the
crab-creature as he let go of the slime-
line and crashed to the
ground. The crowd
cowered in helpless
terror as the white
sheets reared up
with an eerie
rustling sound,
ready to engulf
Danjo.

"No, you don't!"
Zill grabbed one in
her jaws and yanked
it away. Quickly she found
it was as tough and stiff as hard-boiled
bogeys – and tasted even worse. She
spat it out – as another giant tissue
came billowing out of nowhere to land
on her head. "Aargh! Danjo, quick – I
can't see!"

Danjo fired boiling hot slime at Zill's attacker, but the tissue merely absorbed it and continued to attack, lifting her into the air. Before he could fire again, the hostile hankies tightened around him, pinning his pincers to his sides. "This is ridiculous," he groaned. "How can these things be so strong? They wipe noses!"

"Not just noses," Zill gasped as the living tissue slammed her down on the ground. "This one's wiping the floor with me!" She kicked and bit as it hurled her around, and finally tore a hole large enough to push her head through. Instantly the tissue tightened around her throat, choking her.

"Oh, no!" someone yelled as the crowd's cries of panic grew louder still. "Here come the Conks – with more prisoners!"

Helpless in the grip of her nose-wiping nemesis, Zill stared, speechless: four giant walking noses had appeared through gaps in the towering car-cliffs on the far side of the crowd. Ahead of them they herded dozens more terrified monsters – wrapped up in green-stained tissues – onto the rusty racetrack to join the existing scrum. SPLAT! SPLOSH! The Conks blew big green blobs from their nostrils and stuck their prisoners fast.

"Can't . . . let them do this," panted Danjo, still trying to break free.

"Have . . . to stop them."

One of the Conks looked over sharply. "Stop us?" he said in his harsh, bunged-up voice. "No. Interference with the Test Zone will not be tolerated."

"Test Zone?" Zill echoed. "What d'you mean?"

"That is no concern of yours."
Sniffing and snuffling, the Conk
trampled over the poor monsters in the
crowd to reach the Squaddies. "You
cannot stop our plans."

"We'll see about that," said Zill
bravely as the warty monstrosity drew
closer. "The Slime Squad never gives
up."

"This time you will." Coldly, the
Conk surveyed the Squaddies. "You will
be stuck here like everyone else – and
left to rot . . ."

Struggling even harder, but still just as
helpless, Zill and
Danjo could only
watch as the
Conk aimed his
dribbling nostrils
straight at them,
and prepared to
fire . . .

Chapter five

PLANE CRAZY!

Zill and Danjo closed their eyes, ready for the splatting of a lifetime – and suddenly heard a mighty roar of engines just above them . . .

Danjo opened his eyes – and gasped! A white aeroplane was zooming towards them, hugging the ground as if it meant to land.

The Conk glanced up,
astonished – and then
squawked as a metal
wing whacked him
away. He was
propelled high into

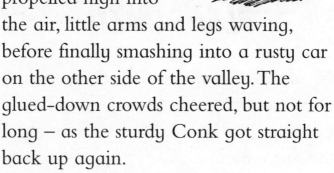

the air, little arms and legs waving,
before finally smashing into a rusty car
on the other side of the valley. The
glued-down crowds cheered, but not for
long – as the sturdy Conk got straight
back up again.

"Where did that plane come
from . . . ?" Zill squinted into the sky,
and gasped to see a familiar furry friend
waving from the cockpit. "Danjo, look –
it's Plog!"

"And check out
who's with him,"
breathed Danjo,
boggling as the
plane turned to
reveal a slender

white-clad arm waving from the pilot's side, with a big red mouth just behind it. "It's . . . Countess Kiss!"

"HUH?" Zill spluttered. "What's going on?"

"Attack that aircraft!" roared the battered Conk. "Bring it down!"

At once, a volley of green splodges sprayed from the nose-monsters on the valley floor. The white plane dipped and dived and looped the loop as it daringly dodged the sticky missiles – then an enormous cloud of thick white fog exploded from its rear end.

"It's been hit!" cried Danjo.

"I don't think so." Through the plane's passenger window Zill saw Plog clapping his hands – and then it turned above them once again. "That must be the smoke that Lip-features used for sky-writing!"

The dense cloud spread out overhead, cloaking the entire valley. Zill held her breath as the trapped crowd burst into helpless coughing. Even the tissue holding Zill began to twitch and splutter – and while it was distracted, she finally kicked her way free. "Danjo," she gasped, "I've got loose!"

"Then now it's my turn." There was some scuffling and the heavy *FWAP!* of fabric slapping the ground. "There!" said Danjo. "The hanky took a spanky!" He took Zill's paw in his pincer and ran

for the icy slime-bridge. "We can't help these poor monsters right now — it's time to beat a neat retreat!"

Zill could hardly see a thing through the smoke. But as she climbed the slippery bridge she could hear the sound of the aeroplane approaching once more, coming closer and closer . . .

"Whoa!" she gasped as strong, bony arms snatched her up, and she was whisked into the air as if she'd jumped aboard some incredible fairground ride.

"Hang on tight," called a familiar husky voice beside her. "It's a long way down."

"Countess Kiss?" Zill gulped and gripped the plane's left wing with all six legs.

From the sound of Danjo's hoots and yells he'd been picked up in much the same way on the other side of the plane – by Plog. "I never thought I'd say this, Countess, but . . . er, thanks."

"You owe me one." Settling back into the cockpit to take the joystick, the countess smiled. "And don't you forget it."

"The Conks are after her, Zill, just like they're after us," said Plog. "For now, at least – we're on the same side. Where's Furp?"

"Trying to get those noses' grotty goo off PIE's sensors," said Danjo, dangling from his pincers. "I guess the Conks didn't want anyone watching while they stuck the Formula Bum crowd to the ground."

"But why would they want to do such a thing?" Plog wondered.

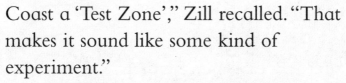

Countess Kiss shrugged. "Maybe they don't like motor racing."

"They called the Car Wreck Coast a 'Test Zone'," Zill recalled. "That makes it sound like some kind of experiment."

"Well, Zill and Danjo, you'd better hang on extra-tight," said Plog. "I want Countess Kiss to sky-write a warning to keep all monsters away from here."

"Are you crazy?" The countess pointed down at the smoky valley. "You saw those Conks firing at us. They're probably bringing in reinforcements."

"We can't let innocent monsters keep blundering into their trap," Plog said firmly. "A quick message, and then we must find Furp."

Zill tried to spy the two tyres that hid PIE's sensor, but it was too smoky. "I only hope he's all right," she murmured.

Under Plog's instruction, Countess Kiss steered her plane this way and that until another message appeared in the skies over the stricken valley:

She was just finishing the final R when a flurry of green sludge shot up through the air and slammed into the underside of the plane.

"Uh-oh – Conks down below!" Danjo hollered.

Zill's eyes widened as she saw more than a dozen of the sinister pointed figures firing from the giant car-wreck clifftops. "We need to get out of here!"

The countess sent the plane swerving and climbing through the sky, trying to get clear. "I told you we were crazy to stay around here!"

Then – SQUELCH! – a humungous green snot-ball engulfed the front of the plane – including the propeller. The engine juddered and roared, but the gunged-up propeller would no longer turn . . .

And the plane began to drop out of the sky.

Plog grabbed Countess Kiss by the shoulder. "Where are the parachutes?"

The countess shook her glossy red head. "There aren't any."

They were diving even more steeply now. "This is *so* not good," said Danjo.

"You could say that." Zill clung onto the wing for dear life. "Or you could say – EEEEEEEEEEK!"

"Our only chance is to touch down in what's left of the Nosepick Ocean," Plog shouted. "Can we reach it?"

"We can try." Countess Kiss gripped the plane's joystick. "Hang on!"

With incredible skill, she forced the dying plane round in a circle, riding the gusting wind as best she could. The three Squaddies could only watch and hope as the plane dipped lower and lower over the rusting landscape. By now, the Nosepick Ocean was little more than a shallow pool of green slush in the bottom of a trash-filled, rocky basin.

Zill groaned. "Is there even enough liquid left to break our fall?"

"We're about to find out," Plog shouted as the gooey ground rushed up to meet them. "Brace yourselves!"

With a breathtaking bang and a spectacular splash, the white plane slammed into what was left of the Nosepick Ocean!

Zill and Danjo were jolted clear by
the impact. They cartwheeled through
the air until – CLANG! – Zill ended up
in a rusty old shopping trolley and –
WHUNCH! – Danjo landed headfirst
in a clump of seaweed.

But they were the lucky ones. As the
plane bounced and scraped across the
gloopy seabed, it struck stones and
boulders and rusting hunks of metal.
Plog and Countess Kiss were squeezed

and scrunched and tangled together in incredible knots until, finally, it screeched to a stop.

"Nice flying," Plog mumbled, his snout squashed into the countess's armpit. "Danjo? Zill? Are you all right?"

There was no reply.

"I was a fool to hope for the Slime Squad's protection," the countess moaned, pulling Plog's tail out of her mouth. "You can't even protect *yourselves*!"

"Stop moping," said Plog crossly, "and start thinking – why are the Conks so keen to catch us?" He tugged his leg out from behind her back and tapped one of his metal boots. "Perhaps it's because we both make some seriously bad smells – and that makes us a danger to them!"

Countess Kiss stared. "You mean, the Conks are scared of that pongy slime your feet make when they're bared to the air?"

Plog nodded. "And I'll bet they hate your breath of death. Giant noses must be super-sensitive to nasty niffs – perhaps *that* is how we can fight them!"

"Uh-oh. It looks as if we might get to test that theory." The lippy lady pointed through the plane's broken windscreen. "We have Conks incoming – from under the seabed!"

Plog felt his heart quicken as he saw a gang of six conk-monsters and two tissues emerge through a hidden hatch in the sludgy ground.

Within seconds they were swarming over the plane – and breaking down the door . . .

Chapter Six

NOSE-GO AREA

KWANG! The plane door was heaved
off its hinges. Plog swapped a helpless
look with Countess Kiss as a hairy
Conk pushed his way inside.

"Now, there is no
escape," the creature
croaked. "You will be
taken to . . . El
Conko."

Countess Kiss
raised her eyebrows.
"El who?"

The sinister schnozz
smiled nastily. "El Conko
– king of Conks!"

70

"Don't think so, sweetie." The countess plumped up her lips. "Get ready for the biggest kiss on the nose *ever* . . ."

"Not yet," hissed Plog. "You heard him: El Conko's their leader – if we get rid of him, perhaps we'll get his hench-noses off our backs too."

"No talking," snapped the Conk. He fired a bogey blast that splattered over Plog's shoulder, knocking him clear of the countess and sticking him to the plane.

"Ow!" Plog complained. "Now, how are you going to take me anywhere?"

The Conk smiled as a large wet tissue squeezed inside and scrubbed roughly at Plog's shoulder. In moments the gunk had melted away – but the tissue wrapped itself around him, pinning his arms to his sides as the Conk yanked him outside with the countess.

"So, there's a way to unstick that stuff," Plog noted. "That's good news for those poor monsters glued to the ground in the valley."

"Hooray," the countess grumbled as a second stained tissue engulfed her. "How can you worry about other monsters at a time like this?"

"I worry about lots of things," said Plog, nodding to what looked like a large plughole beside the hatch in the ground. "Such as, why have the Conks deliberately drained the Nosepick Ocean?"

His question hung in the air as he and the countess were forced to climb down the hatch and into the Conks' gloomy lair . . .

Just a few metres away, hidden by seaweed, Danjo had heard the stomp and squelch of footsteps approaching and woken from his daze – just in time to see Plog and Countess Kiss being pushed underground by the Conks, and the hatch door swing shut behind them.

Unsteadily, he climbed out of the undergrowth – and heard a familiar groan from an upturned shopping trolley close by. "Zill," he hissed. "Are you OK?"

"I feel like my body's been blown to bits and then stitched back together by blind rats with no paws," said Zill. "Otherwise, I'm fine!"

"Plog and Lady Lip-face aren't." Danjo sighed. "They've been caught by the Conks."

Zill shuddered. "Nasty . . . Well, we've already proved we can't tackle those things alone. Let's get back to Furp and the Slime-mobile, and see what PIE thinks."

"He'll have a plan," Danjo agreed,

staring at the twin tyres in the distance. "But the Slime-mobile is miles away, and those Conks we met before will be out for blood."

"Then we'd better take the Catapult Express!" Zill scrambled out of the trolley and spat out a string of slimy strands between two large rocks, making a kind of net. Then she and Danjo backed into it, digging their feet in, stretching it as far as it would go, until . . .

BOINNG! The two Squaddies lifted their legs and were pinged across the ocean plain like stones from a slingshot.

Zill's aim was spot on – and as they came in to land beside the tyres, Danjo sprayed out a heap of soft slush beneath them to cushion their fall.

"Furp?" Zill called, scrambling up. "Funny. There's no sign of him."

"But there *are* signs that a Conk passed this way." Danjo pointed to some green gunk on the black rubber wall, and some tracks in the ground. "It looks like Furp is a prisoner as well as Plog! What are we going to do?"

In the Conks' lair, Plog was asking himself a similar question. He had been forced to climb down a ladder – not easy when you are caught in the grip of a hostile tissue – into a deep, dark metal chamber with a drain in the floor. Once there, the tissue tugged him through a heavy door with a watertight seal.

"It's like something divers might use,"

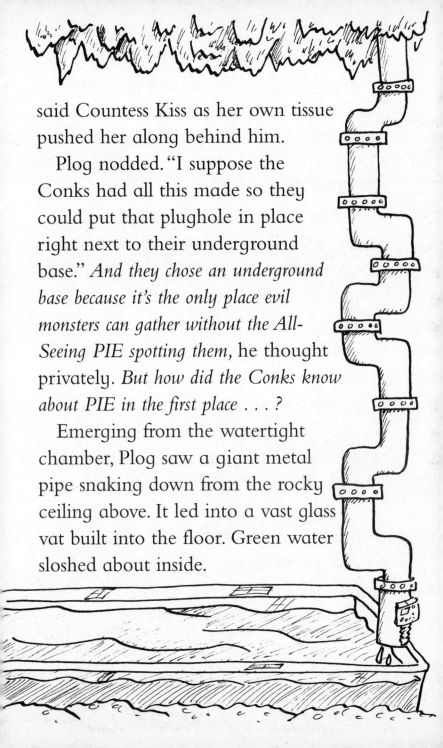

said Countess Kiss as her own tissue
pushed her along behind him.

Plog nodded. "I suppose the
Conks had all this made so they
could put that plughole in place
right next to their underground
base." *And they chose an underground
base because it's the only place evil
monsters can gather without the All-
Seeing PIE spotting them,* he thought
privately. *But how did the Conks know
about PIE in the first place . . . ?*

Emerging from the watertight
chamber, Plog saw a giant metal
pipe snaking down from the rocky
ceiling above. It led into a vast glass
vat built into the floor. Green water
sloshed about inside.

Plog turned to one of his Conk captors. "So you've sucked the entire ocean into there. Why? To make a swimming pool for your pet nose-rags?"

"The Attack Tissues are not pets. They are our disposable slaves, pulled out as required." The Conk snorted. "We have drained away the sea because only the chemicals within it can dissolve our bogeys."

"Like a solvent," said the countess. "Those same chemicals must keep the Nosepick Ocean from turning solid."

Plog stared down at the tissue that held him. "This thing wiped me free in the plane," he recalled. "It must've been

soaked in this solvent stuff."

"Correct," snuffled another Conk. "Now we have total control over its supply."

"No wonder you chose to make the neighbouring coast your Test Zone," said Plog. "That way, no one nearby could get to the ocean-water before you drained it."

"Enough talk," wheezed the Conk. "Move faster!"

The tissues swept Plog and the countess along at a trot. The ground was covered in crusty bogeys, and sloped upwards towards a pair of large green doors – which opened into sudden brightness.

Marvelling, Plog saw a ceiling of smashed glass stretching high overhead, held together by snot and propped up by tall pillars. "We must be under Broken Glass Beach."

"On the other side of the ocean," Countess Kiss agreed.

Sunlight reflected eerily through the glass in shades of bottle green and dirty brown, illuminating a grand and glittering throne room with thick cardboard walls. On a huge chair carved from driftwood and cushioned with handkerchiefs sat a big red nose-monster, the ugliest and meanest-looking Plog had yet seen.

Brown bristles poked out of his nostrils. A fancy lace cape swaddled his body.

Plog felt a tingle of fear as the Attack Tissues forced him and Countess Kiss towards the regal Conk, and the other noses fell to their hairy knees.

"I am El Conko," said the big red nose in a voice that dripped with menace (and a little catarrh). "Rightful

master of Trashland."

"Rightful?" Plog spluttered. "What gives you the right to glue harmless monsters to the ground?"

"And to scare off all the harmful ones?" added Countess Kiss.

"I have *every* right." El Conko smiled unpleasantly. "You see, I am a nose who was once part of a face; a very great and very special face – the face of Trashland's creator, Doctor Godfrey Gunk!"

Chapter Seven

THE GREAT QUEST

"I don't believe it," breathed Plog, staring at the demonic schnozzle on the throne. "You can't be part of Godfrey Gunk. His nose didn't just come to life and hop off his face, did it!"

Countess Kiss seemed baffled. "Godfrey Gunk? Creator of Trashland?"

"That's right." Plog had been told the truth about Trashland's origins by PIE, and quickly

explained. "Gunk was a mad scientist.
He wanted to turn rubbish dumps into
mini monster safari parks. Wanted to
create life. So he did loads of
experiments but none of them worked."

"The Trashland experiment was a
failure," El Conko broke in. "Even when
Doctor Gunk added his
own DNA to his
chemical soup –
skin scrapings
from the side of
his nose – it
made no
difference."

"But Gunk
didn't know
that there was
radioactive stuff
buried in the ground
here," Plog continued. "The
missing ingredient that did what he
could not – bring monsters to life."

"And that's how Trashland was born?" The countess's eyes were full of wonder. "Incredible."

"Incredible? Pah!" The angry El Conko jumped down from his throne. "Trashland was messed up from the start! Even my Conks and I were created by accident, when Doctor Gunk's nose-scrapings mingled with radioactive toxic waste."

"I guess this explains how you knew about PIE." Behind the throne, Plog saw a large, near-empty box of tissues. "How about these nasty nose-rags of yours? Where did they come from?"

"Doctor Gunk was experimenting with intelligent tissues that wipe noses automatically," said the Conk. "We have completed his work – by making them horribly hostile Attack Tissues."

He snarled and snuffled with laughter, sounds that were taken up by his followers in the grand glass chamber. "Soon we shall complete our creator's plans for Trashland. That is our Great Quest."

Plog frowned. "But what Gunk wanted was exactly what we have now – a tip that teems with monstery life."

"NOT TRUE!" boomed El Conko.

"How would you know?" The countess pursed her chapped lips. "Did you ever ask him?"

"They didn't have to," came the voice of a familiar frog-monster. "They found his secret diary."

"Furp!" Plog stared as his friend was swept into sight by another tissue, accompanied by two Conks who held a large scrap of paper carefully between them. "I'm so glad you're all right. Er, you are all right, aren't you?"

Furp looked bruised and bedraggled, his helmet at a wonky angle, the radar dish bent and spinning

slowly. "I've been trapped inside a toxic nostril, dragged halfway across Broken Glass Beach, and taken down here through a secret entrance – none of which was much fun."

He sighed and shook his head. "But then the Conks showed me this scrap from Gunk's diary, thinking it would persuade me to help them in their plans. And now that I *know* their plans, I feel a whole lot worse."

"Furp LeBurp *will* help us in our Great Quest," El Conko declared, glaring at Plog and Countess Kiss. "And so will you two."

"I bet I know what kind of a quest it is too," sneered the countess. "A *conk-quest!*"

Plog nodded. "Just another bunch of nutty villains out to rule Trashland."

"It's worse than that," said Furp gravely. "The Conks want to DESTROY Trashland – and wipe out all monster life!"

"*What?*" Plog whispered in shock.

89

"We MUST do it," El Conko thundered. "That is what our creator wanted. He wrote down his instructions clearly!" He stamped over to the two Conks and snatched away the piece of paper. "Listen to this –
My work is a failure. I will go away and never come back. But first I must destroy the whole experiment – EVERYTHING must be destroyed."

Plog groaned. "But Gunk wrote that when he was really angry, before he knew there was any life here!"

"How dare you question the word of the Creator?" El Conko boomed. "We MUST complete the destruction he began."

Just then, a large, square door in the cardboard wall flipped open. Half a dozen Conks lumbered in and bowed to El Conko. "O Mighty Nose," said one, "we have been forced to call an end to the test. Monsters have stopped coming to the Car Wreck Coast Test Zone."

"They were scared off by the warning in the sky," another added.

Plog smiled at Countess Kiss. "Good."

"But the test was still a success," the first one went on. "Of the two hundred monsters we splatted in the valley, only twelve were able to free themselves. Of the twenty cars we attacked, not one escaped. From the sixty-eight houses we sealed with our snot, only one family made it out through a loose chimney pot."

"Excellent," El Conko declared. "Now we know the true effectiveness of our nose-cement, we shall attack Trashland in force. We will drive the monsters out, or stick them where they stand, or seal them inside their cars or buildings until they starve to death. Then we shall bulldoze their world, until not a single home is left standing." He stood up on his throne, nostrils quivering. "Finally, we will force Furp the clever chemist to mix up a super-deadly concoction that will poison the entire rubbish dump.

Never again will Trashland be able to support life!"

"Even by my standards, that's pretty low," said Countess Kiss. "I mean, what happens to you?"

"We shall die too, of course," said El Conko proudly. "Our work will be done."

Plog turned to the countess. "I think it's time we put our pongy plan into action," he growled. "Frankly, El Conko and his schnozz brigade are getting *right up my nose!*"

Defying the tissue that held him, Plog kicked out his legs like a can-can dancer. His wet metal boots flew off across the throne room and El Conko stared as, almost immediately, thick, putrid slime began to pour from Plog's toes. A shocking reek of yucky feet filled the air.

"There!" Plog smiled wickedly. "How d'you *nose*-hoppers like that?"

"And now it's my turn." Before the stunned Conks could react, Countess Kiss used her sharp claws to tear through her own tissue and grabbed hold of El Conko. "Come here, handsome – and let me plant a killer kiss on you!"

"That's the way, you two!" cried Furp excitedly, watching Plog flick yellow toe-jam all around the throne room.

"Noses that size must be super-sensitive. When they're forced to sniff such a powerful pong they'll—"

"LOVE IT!" bellowed El Conko, pushing Countess Kiss away as the last Attack Tissue in his personal box floated out to grab her. "Mmmm! I knew capturing you was a good idea." He got down on his knees and happily sniffed the foot-slime on the floor. "And you too, Plog. What a delicious niff! What a heaven-sent scent!"

"I . . . I don't get it," Plog gasped as his tissue forced him back into his boots and propelled him forward to join Countess Kiss, leaving the other Conks to swoon at the slime-stains he'd left on the floor. "We thought you wanted to catch us because you were scared of our smells."

"Fool!" El Conko hissed as he rose to his hairy feet. "We *wanted* your smells. We prize them above all others –

because a horrible pong makes our snot twice as STRONG! And with such powers, our Great Quest cannot fail."

A sudden sniffing noise started up in the passage behind Furp. It sounded like one of the conk-creatures, only ten times as loud. And whatever was making it was coming closer.

"Uh-oh," Furp murmured, and even his tissue guard trembled. "What's that?"

El Conko smiled. "It would take far too long to splat every monster in Trashland on our own – the population might work together to defeat us. Luckily, a few of Doctor Gunk's nose-scrapings fell near some *very* toxic waste indeed . . . and created a mutant masterpiece of sinister super-nature!"

Plog gulped, Countess Kiss boggled
and Furp jumped into the air as a
gigantic, pinkish-green Conk-monster
came waddling in on ten pairs of short,
fat, hairy legs. Its nostrils were huge
black holes, trailing thick black hairs. It
had only one eye, big and bloodshot,
perched on the broad bridge of its
bumpy, lumpy body.

"Behold, the Special Weapons Nose!"
cried El Conko. "Soon to be the
ultimate destroyer of all Trashland!"

Chapter Eight
NOT TO BE SNIFFED AT

Plog stared in dismay at the Special Weapons Nose. Even the other Conks looked afraid as it lurched ever closer. "That thing is reeeeeee-volting!"

"And completely deadly," El Conko gloated. "It can fire bogeys as big as a bungalow, and make enough snot to smother skyscrapers." He leered at Plog and Countess Kiss.

"Once it has fully absorbed the horrific stinks you two can make, its nose-goo will be twenty times as strong. Trashland will be slimed to a standstill, and then levelled to the ground – and the Conks will stand triumphant!"

"Furp," cried Plog, "we've got to do something . . ." He trailed off. "Furp?"

The Special Weapons Nose was lurching closer, but of the frog-monster there was no sign. The tissue-guard who'd held him was now quaking on the floor, apparently overcome with terror.

"Curse these disposable Attack Tissues!" El Conko raged. "They wear out too quickly on victims with superpowers. Now I'll have to open a fresh box . . ."

"Plog, look!" Countess Kiss pointed to the large square door last used by the Test Zone Conks: it stood ajar. "Your friend has run off and left us."

"Furp wouldn't do that," Plog insisted.

"Whatever he's up to, he won't get far." El Conko signalled to the Test Zone Conks. "Pursue Furp LeBurp. Bring him back at once."

As the Conks saluted and scuttled off to obey, El Conko stomped over to the tissue who'd been Furp's former captor and kicked it. "You gutless rag! You know the punishment for failure . . ." He whistled to the Special Weapons Nose.

The monstrous beast sent out a long hair from its nostril, grabbed the tissue, and then sucked it inside.

Nasty chewing noises soon followed, and Plog cringed.

"Is that what will happen to us?" asked Countess Kiss shakily.

"Nothing so quick," hissed El Conko. "You will be sniffed inside and stuck in the Special Weapons Nose's nostrils until he has sucked all the stink out of you. Only then will you be chewed and swallowed."

"Furp had the right idea," said the Countess gloomily, "escaping like that."

But suddenly the square door opened a crack, and Furp hopped merrily through. "Hello again! Sorry for popping out. Have I missed anything?"

The Special Weapons Nose rumbled ominously, and El Conko's horrid features twisted in fury. "I sent my Conks to catch you. How did you avoid them?"

"Oh, quite easily." Furp hopped onto a pillar and climbed to the top with his slimy hands and feet. "To be honest, I think your Conks are feeling a bit run down – or should I say, run *over*!"

All at once Plog heard the muffled roar of a powerful engine – and then a barely-visible blur smashed down the door and burst into the throne room.

"The Slime-mobile!" he cheered. "Here to save us in the nick of time!"

"The radar dish on my helmet detected that the Slime-mobile was close by," Furp yelled. "I knew Zill and Danjo must be out looking for us – so I thought I'd better hop outside and show them the hidden way into the Conk base!"

"Brilliant! I knew you hadn't run away." With sudden hope lending him fresh strength, Plog pushed out his chest and tore his tissue captor in two. "Countess, get ready to jump aboard!"

"I can't," Countess Kiss groaned, struggling against the white sheet that held her. "This fresh tissue may be soft, but by golly, it's strong!"

"You cannot escape!" bellowed El Conko. He fired green globs at Plog, who dived for cover behind the throne. Meanwhile, pillars and Conks were smashed aside as the Slime-mobile sped about, turning tightly this way and that.

The Special Weapons Nose sniffed and snorted as if tracking the truck by scent alone, and raised its enormous bulk, ready to fire. SPLAMM! SPLUTT! Titanic twin explosions of super-sticky sludge erupted from its mighty nostrils. There was a squeal of brakes as the Slime-mobile changed course and bashed into El Conko! The bogey blast struck the wall instead, almost knocking it down.

"Careful where you fire!" El Conko bawled groggily. "Do you want to bring the Broken Glass Beach down on our heads?"

Plog sighed with relief as the Slime-mobile pulled up beside him and Danjo threw open the door. "Did someone order a taxi?"

"Get us out of here!" cried Furp, then jumped down onto the Slime-mobile's invisible roof and swung himself inside. "Come on, Plog!"

Plog threw the still-struggling countess over his shoulder. "Don't worry," he told her, "we'll get you free of this snotty straitjacket."

But then a nostril-hair snaked out from the Special Weapons Nose and quickly wound

itself around Countess Kiss's bare feet.
With a hungry bellow, it yanked her
right out of Plog's grasp! Kicking and
screaming, the countess was dragged
across the throne-room floor towards the
humungous nose.

"Countess!" Plog gasped. He was
about to chase after her when a second
nose-hair came shooting out towards
him.

Danjo quickly grabbed Plog and
hauled him inside the Slime-mobile.
Immediately Zill floored the accelerator
and the monster-truck shot off through
the square exit, heading for the surface.

"Glad to have you back!" called Zill.

"But what about Countess Kiss?" Plog shook his head sadly. "She'll be stuck inside the Special Weapons Nose. I know she's been bad in the past, but we can't just leave her there, all alone!"

"We've got troubles of our own!" Furp pointed through the windscreen. "Those Test Zone Conks Zill knocked down on the way here – they're back on their feet."

"And they can hear us coming!" Danjo realized.

Plog saw a gang of twelve Conks blocking the passage ahead. High-powered splats shot from their nostrils, smothering their path in bubbling gunk.

"That stuff will stop us in our tracks," Furp cried.

"Hey, Danjo," Zill yelled as the Slime-mobile zoomed closer to the sticky puddle. "What happens if I turn turbo-mode to full power?"

"Dunno." Danjo grinned. "But I can't wait to find out!"

"Here goes . . ." Zill twisted the button, and with a WHOOSH of rocket jets the Slime-mobile shot forward, so fast it left the ground!

"Whoaaa!" Plog, Furp and Danjo were thrown around like wasps in a whirlwind as their vehicle went soaring over the snot-puddle and the Conks in its path, before landing with a clattering, shattering *ker-CRASH!*

"Awesome!" Danjo clapped his pincers together. "What a ride!"

"And here's Broken Glass Beach, dead ahead." Zill steered the Slime-mobile out of the tunnel into the sunlit, sharp-edged landscape. "Let's just hope we don't get a puncture."

"Zill, Danjo, that was a fine rescue." Furp sank down against his lab bench. "But what are we going to do now? We may have escaped the Conks, but we can't stop them. Their assault on Trashland could start at any moment."

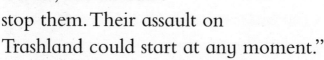

"What's more, Countess Kiss's bog-awful breath is making that jumbo schnozzle stronger all the time," said Plog. "We need to get her out of there for our *own* sake as much as hers. But how?"

"The Nosepick Ocean unsticks their nose-goo," Furp mused. "That's why they've locked all its waters away in that giant underground tank. If we could only get hold of some, we'd be able to free their victims."

"But we can't get hold of any, can we?" Zill muttered. "There's nothing left on the surface."

Suddenly a loud, gurgly rumble sounded from Danjo's tum. "Sorry" – he shrugged – "Furp's mucking about with those silly human spices meant we skipped breakfast this morning, remember?"

"I'd forgotten that," breathed Plog. "Breakfast . . ." He clapped his hands together. "Yes, of course, that's the answer!"

"Huh?" Zill was puzzled. "You want to invite El Conko round for cockroach legs on toast?"

"Not exactly." Plog grinned round at his friends. "I want you and Danjo to hand me and Furp back to the Conks as quickly as possible – ideally before El Conko cracks open a new box of attack tissues."

"Surrender, you mean?" spluttered Furp. "My dear Plog, are you feeling all right in the head?"

"It's the feeling in my snout I'm thinking of," said Plog.

"Well, I hope you *nose* what you're doing, Fur-boy," Zill sighed. "Because this could be the last thing you'll ever do!"

Chapter Nine
SURRENDER!

Back in the throne room, El Conko was gathering his Conk strike-force around him. There were twenty of the mutant hooters in all, sniffing, snorting and snuffling.

They did not make a pretty sight.

The Special Weapons Nose sat in a corner, slurping on Countess Kiss like a baby with a dummy – only her feet could be seen sticking out of his right nostril.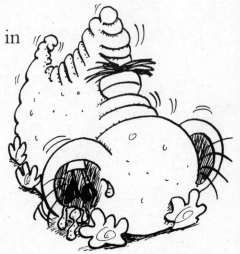

The tough Test Zone Conks looked a bit bruised after their smash-up with the Slime-mobile, but were otherwise unharmed. The rest of the nose-monsters stood there, pink and oily, gazing at their leader with adoring eyes.

"The Slime Squad have escaped," El Conko growled at the assembled Conks. "They will warn Trashland's monsters of our coming attack – so we must strike at once!"

The assembled Conks honked their approval.

"But, El Conko," said the burly schnozz who'd led the attack on Plog and Countess Kiss in Spare Part Canyon, "don't we need Plog's foot-slime to boost the Special Weapons Nose's powers to the maximum – and Furp's powers of chemistry to ensure that no life will ever return to Trashland?"

"We will recapture them soon enough," said El Conko. "The Slime Squad are bound to try to stop our attack – and we shall CRUSH them!"

Just then, the sound of someone clearing his throat carried from the square doorway. The Conks turned as one . . . and found Zill and Danjo peeping into the room!

117

"Er, sorry to interrupt," called Zill. She held a trailing slime-line in her front paws. "We'd like to talk to you."

"You dare to return to the Palace of Conks?" El Conko snorted, and his band of Conk-brothers sniffed in outrage. "You are more foolish than I thought."

"We *were* foolish, trying to fight you," Danjo said quickly. "But Plog believes that if we help you, you'll let us live."

El Conko glared at the Squaddies. "Does he, now?"

Danjo reached back through the doorway and picked up Furp by the scruff of the neck. The frog-monster seemed asleep, dangling limply from his friend's crimson pincer. At the same time, Zill tugged on her slime-strand and Plog shuffled out from round the corner. The sticky rope was wrapped round and round his middle, and a blob of Danjo's slime-ice sat on the end of his nose.

At the sight of their former captives, the Conks started to snarl.

"So!" hissed El Conko. "The Slime Squad surrenders to the power of the Conks."

"Furp and I will do whatever you want," said Plog, sounding bunged up with the ice on his nose. "As long as you promise to let Danjo and Zill get away with the All-Seeing PIE before the destruction starts."

"You want me to promise, Plog?" El Conko sniggered. "Well then, I promise to punish you and Furp for trying to escape. I promise to destroy Zill and Danjo for the trouble they have caused. And I promise to smash PIE to smithereens just as our Creator thought he had done – sensor by sensor." He flared his roomy nostrils. "Get them, my Conks! Ruin and death to those who defy us!"

The enraged killer Conks swarmed

and snuffled across the throne room. Even the Special Weapons Nose took an interest, rising from the ground, its one free nostril twitching.

Zill quickly stuck a peg on her nose. "You were right, Fur-boy. Here come the Conks to get us, just as you predicted."

Still gripped in Danjo's pincer, Furp opened one eye and stuffed cotton wool up his nostrils.

"Well, I'm as ready as I'll ever be."

"And so am I," said Danjo, before holding his breath.

"Good luck, you lot," said Plog, checking his snout was still frozen as the Conks charged ever closer. "Operation 'Bless You' is GO!"

121

And suddenly Danjo hurled Furp
through the air, over the heads of the
charging noses. At the same split-second,
Zill yanked hard on her slime-line; it
unwound from around Plog's middle
and sent him spinning into the ranks of
the charging Conks at super-fast speed.

And as he spun and scattered his nosy foes, a fine dark dust flew out of his fur in all directions. The same fine dark dust that was already sprinkling through strategic holes drilled into Furp's metal pants . . .

The effect of this powder on the Conks was astounding. They stopped in their tracks. Their eyes flickered shut. They took uncertain breaths, sniffing and choking and reeling in all directions. Even the Special Weapons Nose began to twitch as Furp sailed overhead, and the soggy countess up his nostril began to kick her legs.

"What's wrong with you all?" boomed El Conko as Furp landed on a nearby pillar and shook his pants over the throne. "*Attack! Attack! A . . . Ahh . . . AAA-TISH-OOOO!*"

The regal Conk sneezed so hard he sprayed green gloop all over his own feet – gluing himself to the floor. "No!" he shouted, struggling to lift his hairy legs from the unpleasant puddle. "Release me, one of you . . . Ahhh-CHOOO!"

But his sneeze, like his cry for help, went unheeded. Because, all around him, his Conks were sneezing uncontrollably too! Huge, juddering, shuddering sneezes that sent bogeys bursting from their nostrils at a billion miles an hour. The Special Weapons Nose's single eye was gummed shut by slimy drizzle from the neighbouring noses.

"What's happening?" El Conko groaned, his eyes running, his lumpy pink body turning puce as he sneezed yet again. "*What?*"

"You wanted Plog and Furp," Zill yelled, grinning with delight in the doorway, "so we gave them to you. We just happened to roll them in a big bowl of pepper first!"

"Plus we threw in a few other human spices just for fun," called Danjo, whipping up an icy-slime shield to deflect the projectile snot. "Funny-sounding stuff – chilli powder, cumin, paprika . . ."

"In other words – instant sneezing powder!" Plog stopped spinning and shook the last of the dust from his fur. "It's impossible for anyone to fight while they're sneezing – especially nasty giant noses like you!"

The throne room was heaving with jostling Conks, emptying their nostrils all over the place. Zill huddled for shelter behind Danjo's shield. "We'll be stuck for sure if we hang around," she cried.

Danjo nodded. "Ain't that the truth –
let's head for the roof!"

The two Squaddies shinned up a
pillar, out of range of the Conks' flying
snot.

Furp hopped over to join them.
"Plog's plan is working. They're sneezing
themselves silly and sticking each other
to the floor!"

"Hey, Plog!" Danjo shouted, squirting icy slush all over the throne-room floor like a big crimson sprinkler. "If you walk on my guck, you won't get stuck!"

"Nice one, Danjo!" Plog skated over the icy floor, past the impotent Conks, making for the blinded Special Weapons Nose.

It was quivering and quavering but it still hadn't sneezed. "Countess Kiss, are you all right?"

"Do I look all right to you?" came the indignant reply.

"You don't *sound* too bad." Plog yanked and tugged on the slender legs poking out of the giant nose. "Now, let's get you out."

But then the Special Weapons Nose finally tore open its eyelid and glared down at Plog. "FEEEEEET," it boomed. "HUNGRYYYYYYY!" Flexing its free nostril, it breathed in sharply.

And, to his horror, Plog found himself being sucked inside!

Chapter Ten

THE CONKS' FINAL BLOW

"Hey!" As he was drawn ever closer to the hideous hairy nostril, Plog waved to his friends. "A little help here?"

"On the case, Fur-boy!" Zill and Danjo wolf-whistled at the Special Weapons Nose at ear-splitting volume. "Hey! Big nose!"

Distracted, the conk-creature tilted upward to look at them – just as Furp turned an athletic somersault and

released a huge
cloud of
sneezing powder
from his pants.
In seconds, the
monster had
sucked it all up.
"Argghh,"
groaned the Special
Weapons Nose,
wriggling and winking, twitching and
twotching, hovering on the brink of
what had to be a truly colossal sneeze.
"Ahh . . . ahhhh . . . AHHH . . ."

"No!" bellowed El Conko, already
half buried in bogeys. "Special Weapons
Nose, I forbid you to sneeze! You'll
bring the entire palace down on top
of us!"

Zill and Danjo dropped down beside
Plog, and Furp joined them with an
anxious gulp. "I'm afraid El Conko may
be right!"

"AHHHH . . ." The Special Weapons Nose was shaking like a volcano about to erupt. "*AHHHHHH . . .*"

"Time to leave," said Plog breathlessly. "But there are too many Conks between us and the exit." He pointed to a goop-covered wall behind them. "We'll have to take those green double-doors – the passage that connects this place to the hatch in the bottom of the Nosepick Ocean. Furp, Danjo, get going – make sure the way is clear."

"Gotcha," said Danjo, speeding off with Furp.

"*AHHHHHH . . .*" The Special Weapons Nose had begun to shiver uncontrollably. "*AHHHHHH-HH . . .*"

"Don't!" El Conko begged his gigantic servant. "Please, don't!"

"Stand by to snag Countess Kiss with a slime-line, Zill," Plog told her. "You'll only get one chance."

Zill nodded nervously. "She saved me before. I'll do my best for her."

And then, finally—

"*AHHHHHHH-CHOOOOOOOOOOOOOOOOO!!!*"

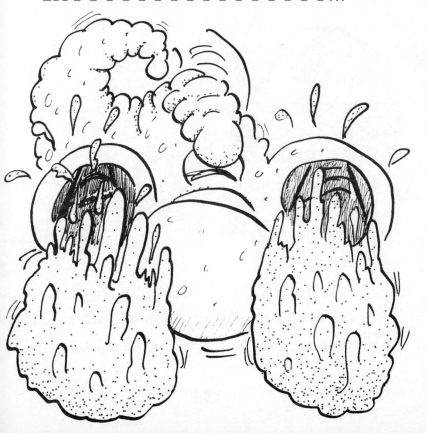

With a sound like an express train
thundering into an earthquake, the
Special Weapons Nose sneezed at last!
The throne room shook. Pillars
crumbled. The glass in the ceiling rattled
and cracked. Out shot the snotty
countess, still in the grip of the rope-
like nose-hair. It held her tightly
in mid air while the storm
of nose-gloop raged
around her . . .

And a second was all Zill needed.
The feisty poodle-skunk spat out a
slime-line, snagged the countess's ankle,

then yanked on it with all her strength. Countess Kiss was tugged clean out of her raincoat as Zill swung her round in a half-circle and straight into Plog's waiting arms.

"OOF!" Plog almost fell over under the gloopy countess's weight. "It's all right. I've got you."

The countess peered up at him, blinking in the sudden light. "I . . . I can't believe you came back for me."

"I told you" – Plog shrugged – "the Slime Squad  help any monster in trouble."

"So we'd better help ourselves," Zill said sharply as the Special Weapons Nose sneezed again—

"KER-CHOOOOOO!"

This time, green goo gushed out of both nostrils as if sprayed from a fire-fighter's hose. The trapped noses in the throne room groaned and gargled as they were doused in the disgusting stuff. Even the Special Weapons Nose himself was stuck fast in his own slime.

Suddenly broken glass began to fall from the roof.

"Noooooooooo," sobbed El Conko. "Our Great Quest cannot end like this . . ."

"Sorry, Conks," called Plog. "I'm afraid that just like anyone else with a nose – you've blown it!"

"Come on!" Zill shouted as a further phenomenal sneeze from the colossal conk-monster sent a revolting wave of gloop sloshing towards them. "If that stuff so much as touches us, we'll be trapped here with the Conks."

Plog led the charge for the exit, the countess still in his arms. "You can put me down now," she said.

"I wish I could," groaned Plog. "With that gunk all over you, you're stuck to my fur!"

"Goes to show," Zill panted, "that this whole situation is too close for comfort!"

They sprinted down the gloomy tunnel, desperate to outrun the raging river of slime surging after them. At last Plog saw the metal chamber through which he'd entered – and Danjo, standing there in front of it.

"I've smashed open the hatchway to the surface," he shouted.

"And I've found the marine-machine that sucked the Nosepick Ocean into this vat," said Furp. Clinging to the side of the pipe above the vast glass tank, he was feverishly dismantling a control panel. "If I can reverse the systems, it will pump the sea back out into its normal place . . ."

"And we can use the water to unstick those poor monsters on the Car Wreck Coast!" Zill realized.

"Not to mention me and the countess," said Plog as Danjo helped them into the metal vault and pushed them up the ladder towards the fresh air.

"Quickly, Furp!" Zill climbed the ladder at record speed. "There's a tidal wave of snot on its way here!"

"Just a few seconds more," Furp muttered. Like a stream of molten lava, the noxious nose-goo came bubbling round the corner,

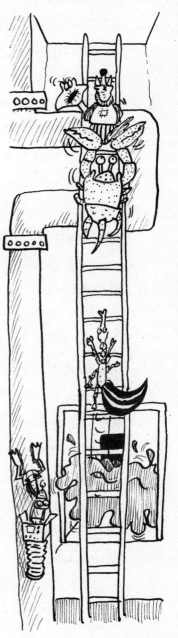

swallowing all in its path. "Let's try it now . . ." He slammed down a lever and, at the last possible moment, leaped into the vault and sprang out through the hatch to safety.

SPLOOOOSH! The wave crashed into the vat, and Danjo slammed the metal hatch cover closed.

"We did it!" gasped Zill. "We got out!"

"But the entire Nosepick Ocean is about to be forced out through the Conks' plughole," Furp reminded them. "So, get ready to swim." A huge, yellow-green fountain burst out of the plughole, refilling the rocky basin at dizzying speed. "Swim for your lives!"

Suddenly the

Squaddies and
Countess Kiss were
swept away by the
churning liquid. Plog was
thrown clear of the countess
as the gunk that bound them
was swiftly dissolved.

Must keep going, he told
himself, arms and legs aching,
holding his breath as the lumpy
water seethed and bubbled
around him. *I must . . . I
MUST . . .*

Then the ocean's onslaught was
suddenly over. Plog popped up
close to the Car Wreck Coast,
and quickly gulped down the
wonderful whiffy air. Furp,
Zill and Danjo helped him
wade ashore – just as the
sound of breaking glass
cut sharply across the
newly formed ocean.

Plog stared across the sea and saw that part of the Broken Glass Beach had collapsed and caved in, not far from where they'd left the Slime-mobile.

"There goes the Conks' lair," Furp murmured. "Sealed shut for ever."

"And good riddance!" Danjo added.

"Hey," said Zill, looking around. "What happened to Countess Kiss?"

"I'm right here," came a familiar purr, and they saw the countess crawling wearily onto the shore beside them. "And – though it hurts me to say it –

thanks for saving my life."

"That's OK, Countess," said Plog.
"But just promise me one thing."

"I know, I know." The countess held
up a hand to stop him. "You want me
to give up my life of crime. Well, all
right. I will. Especially since there's no
one left to team up with now all the
bad guys have moved out of
Trashland!" She shook herself down.
"I'll go back to being a boring old
dentist in the Gunk Glaciers again –
satisfied?"

"Er . . . yes!" said Plog cheerily. "Especially since I was only going to ask you never to write in the sky that we smooched, ever again!"

"Oh, but I *love* to kiss and tell, Ploggy-woggy." Countess Kiss winked and waved goodbye.

"Ta-ta for now," she said, and then strode off towards the grubby Gunk Glaciers.

"Well, bless my gonkberries," said Furp. "With the Conks gone and Countess Kiss turning over a new leaf . . ."

"There isn't a criminal left in Trashland!" Zill marvelled.

"Wow." Danjo frowned. "What will we do with ourselves?"

"What the Slime Squad always used to do before the first evil monsters appeared," said Plog. "We'll make this wild and whiffy rubbish dump world of ours an even better place to live in – by helping monsters in need wherever we find them."

"There's an awful lot of them in the Conks' Test Zone," Danjo reminded them.

Zill nodded. "Now the ocean's come back, we can start unsticking them."

"And we can fix PIE's sensors too," Furp agreed. "Let him know that everything's all right."

"Yes, it really *is* all right," said Plog happily. "And from now on, it always will be." He grinned at his team-mates.

"How's this for a new motto – *Let fear disappear, let wickedness quail . . .* "

Zill, Furp and Danjo joined in to complete Plog's rhyme: "*The Slime Squad are here – and we NEVER fail!*"

THE END

READ THE FIRST EVER SLIME SQUAD STORY!

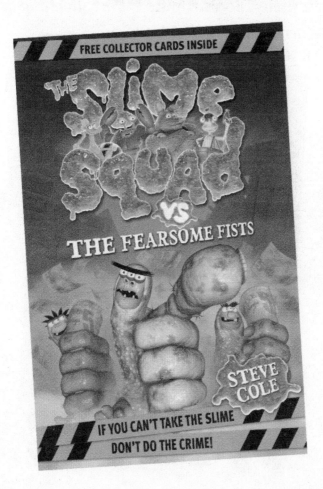

Out now!

DON'T MISS THIS INCREDIBLE SLIME SQUAD ADVENTURE!

Out now!